Perfectly Princess

Purple Princess Wins the Prize

by Alyssa Crowne

illustrated by Charlotte Alder

Scholastic Inc.

New York   Toronto   London   Auckland
Sydney   Mexico City   New Delhi   Hong Kong

Many thanks to my editor,
Shannon Penney,
for making each book sparkle and shine.

ISBN: 978-0-545-16078-0

Text copyright © 2010 by Pure West Productions, Inc.
Illustrations copyright © 2010 by Scholastic Inc.

12 11 10 9 8 7 6 5 4 3 2 1   10 11 12 13 14 15/0

Printed in the U.S.A.   40
Designed by Kevin Callahan
First printing, April 2010

Contents

Chapter One

Storm the Castle!

"'Once upon a time, there was a princess named Crystal,'" Isabel Dawson read out loud. "'Crystal lived in a beautiful castle.'"

Isabel looked at the picture of the castle in her book. It was made of stone and had lots of towers. Princess Crystal was looking out of a window.

"That's a nice castle," Isabel said to herself. "But it's too bad she doesn't have a *purple* castle, like mine!"

Isabel looked around her own castle and smiled. It was made out of her bunk beds! She had a room all to herself, so she only needed one bed. Isabel slept on the top bunk. Her dad had taken out the bed on the bottom. Her mom had hung a purple curtain in front of the space. Then Isabel had filled it with everything a castle needed.

There were comfy purple pillows on the floor. A small bookshelf held Isabel's favorite books. On the top shelf, Isabel had carefully placed her collection of princess figures. They looked like tiny statues. Most of the princesses wore purple dresses, because that was Isabel's favorite color in the whole world.

Finally, her dad had attached a lamp to the wall so Isabel could read inside her castle. She loved to read—especially books about princesses. Princesses always

wore beautiful clothes. They had magical adventures. And they all lived happily ever after!

Isabel's big brothers, Alex and Marco, thought she was weird for reading so much. They liked to tease her.

"Izzy is a nerd!" they would chant. "Dizzy Izzy!"

Isabel didn't mind being called a nerd. But she *hated* being called Izzy. She couldn't imagine a princess named Izzy!

Inside her castle, Isabel felt safe. Nobody in her castle called her Izzy.

Isabel snuggled down into the purple pillows and started to read again. The book about Princess Crystal was called *The Magic Jewel*. Princess Crystal was bored

with being a princess. She wanted to have an adventure! Then one day a fairy came to Princess Crystal's room and asked her to go on a quest for a magic jewel.

"Quest?" Isabel asked out loud. She didn't know that word. She took the dictionary from her shelf and looked it up.

"'A quest is a search or a journey,'" Isabel read out loud. That made sense. The fairy wanted Princess Crystal to search for the magic jewel.

Knock! Knock! Knock!

Somebody was banging on Isabel's door.

"Go away!" Isabel yelled.

"But I have to ask you something." It was one of her big brothers, Alex.

"I'm busy!" Isabel shouted back.

She heard the door open. "Then I'll just have to storm the castle!" Alex cried.

He pulled open the purple curtain. "Ha, found you!" he yelled. He quickly grabbed a princess figure from her shelf and ran away. "Can't catch me!"

"Alex, give that back!" Isabel called. She threw down the book and raced after her brother.

Alex darted into the room he shared with Marco, their oldest brother. Isabel was right behind him. Marco sat on his bed, playing a video game. He acted like he didn't see them.

Alex jumped on his bed, higher and higher. He held the princess figure up over his head. "You can't get it!" he teased.

"Give that back!" Isabel shouted. She threw her arms around Alex, tackling him. They both tumbled onto the floor.

Isabel reached out to grab the princess figure. Alex rolled out of the way. *Bam!*

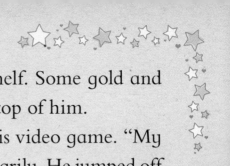

He slammed into a shelf. Some gold and silver trophies fell on top of him.

Marco put down his video game. "My trophies!" he yelled angrily. He jumped off the bed and ran into the hallway. "Izzy, you're in big trouble. I'm telling Mom!"

Chapter Two

No Trophies for Isabel

Before Isabel could say anything, Mrs. Dawson came into the room. Marco stood right behind her.

"Look what she did, Mom!" Marco said, pointing to the trophies. "She knocked them all over!"

"They're my trophies too," Alex added.

"Alex started it," Isabel protested. "He came into my room and stormed my castle. Then he took one of my princesses."

Isabel spotted the toy on the floor. She had always liked it because the princess held a tiny bluebird in her hand. But now the bird had broken off.

Isabel picked it up. "Look! He broke her!"

Mrs. Dawson shook her head. "It seems to me that you're both wrong," she said. "Alex, you should not have taken Isabel's toy. And Isabel, if you have a problem with your brothers, you need to tell me or Dad. Chasing Alex was not a smart idea. Now please apologize to each other."

Isabel sighed. "Sorry, Alex."

"Sorry, Izzy," Alex mumbled.

"Do NOT call me Izzy!" Isabel said loudly.

Their mother shook her head. "You two are impossible," she said. "Please pick up the trophies and give each other some space."

Isabel scooped up the trophies as quickly as she could. Alex was helping, but he was moving very slowly. Isabel just knew he was doing it to bug her.

This is so unfair! Isabel thought. Sometimes she wished she didn't have any brothers at all. Isabel was seven, Alex was nine, and Marco was eleven. The only thing they had in common was that they all had curly dark hair and big, brown eyes.

Besides that, Isabel thought it was hard to believe they were related at all. Alex and Marco didn't like to read. They didn't

like purple. And their bedroom was messy! The walls were covered with cut-out magazine pictures of baseball players.

Isabel liked sports too, but not as much as her brothers. They played soccer in fall, basketball in winter, baseball in spring, and joined the swim team in the summer. Every time they played anything, they got a trophy. At least, it seemed that way.

Isabel put the last trophy on the shelf. "There, I'm done," she said. She looked at Alex. "Now please stay out of my room!"

"You stay out of *our* room," Alex retorted. "Leave our trophies alone!"

Marco looked up from his game. "Don't worry, Alex. Isabel is just jealous of our trophies."

"You're right!" Alex said. "She doesn't have any trophies, just a bunch of books. And princesses."

"Books and princesses are better than trophies!" Isabel cried. She stomped back to her room without another word.

She looked around her castle. Marco was right. She didn't have any trophies at all. In fact, she had never won a prize for anything!

Isabel crawled into her castle and put the princess figure back on the shelf. She placed the broken little bird next to her.

"Don't worry," she said. "I'll fix you with glue."

Isabel felt kind of sad. But it wasn't because of the broken bird. It was because she had never won a prize.

She sighed. "Maybe I'll get one someday," she said. She curled

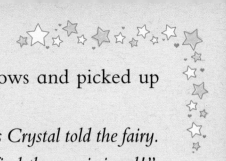

up on her purple pillows and picked up
The Magic Jewel.

"I will do it!" Princess Crystal told the fairy.
"I will go on a quest to find the magic jewel!"

Isabel read the words again, out loud.
Suddenly, she had an idea.

"I will go on my *own* quest," she said.
"But I won't search for a magic jewel.
I, Isabel Dawson, will go on a quest to
win a prize!"

Chapter Three

The Quest Begins

A little while later, Isabel marched downstairs. She found her mom in the backyard, pulling weeds in the flower garden. She had a floppy straw hat on top of her curly hair. Isabel sat in the grass next to her.

"Did you and Alex put away those trophies?" her mom asked.

"Yes," Isabel said. "Mom, I have a question."

Mrs. Dawson used her scissors to cut

a flower with purple petals. She smiled and tucked the flower into Isabel's curls. "What's up, my purple princess?" she asked.

Isabel took a deep breath.

"I want to go on a quest," she announced.

"Will you be gone a long time?" Mrs. Dawson asked. "You have to finish your homework before Monday."

"Mom, I'm serious!" Isabel said. "I want to go on a quest to win a prize. I've never won a prize in my whole life."

"Isabel, you're only seven," her mom said. "You have plenty of time to win a prize."

"But Alex and Marco aren't much older than me, and they have lots of trophies,"

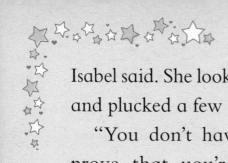

Isabel said. She looked down at the ground and plucked a few blades of grass.

"You don't have to win a prize to prove that you're awesome, Isabel," her mom said. "I already think you're awesome."

Isabel rolled her eyes a little. "I just want to try!"

Mrs. Dawson looked thoughtful. "You could join the swim team this summer," she said. "You're old enough now."

"But summer is far away," Isabel pointed out.

Isabel's mom took off her gardening gloves. "Tell you what. Let's look in the school newsletter. Sometimes they announce contests in there."

Isabel smiled.

Soon, she and her mom were sitting at the kitchen table. Isabel poured two glasses

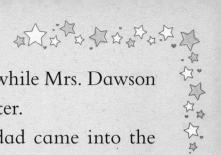

of lemonade for them while Mrs. Dawson opened up the newsletter.

Just then, Isabel's dad came into the room. Mr. Dawson had brown hair. He wasn't short, and he wasn't tall either. He wore blue shorts and a white shirt with a collar. He had a coach's whistle around his neck.

"I'm taking Marco and Alex to soccer practice," he announced. He gave Isabel and her mom each a kiss on the cheek. "What are you two doing?"

"I'm planning my quest," Isabel said proudly.

"Sounds interesting! Tell me about it at dinner, okay?" he said as he headed outside.

Mrs. Dawson pointed to one story in the newsletter. "Field Day is next month," she said. "They give out prizes."

"What is Field Day, again?" Isabel asked.

"That's when students compete in races and other games," her mom explained. "You didn't go last year because you had a bad cold, remember?"

Isabel nodded. "Right! Do you really think I could win a prize there?"

"You're a fast runner," her mom said. "You could enter a running race."

Isabel grinned. She *was* a fast runner. Maybe winning a prize wouldn't be so hard after all!

"I'll do it," she said. "But a month is a long time to wait. Is there anything sooner?"

Mrs. Dawson shook her head. "So impatient, daughter," she teased. "Let's look some more."

She turned the page. Then she hit her forehead with her hand. "Of course! The Cupcake Contest!"

Isabel read from the page: "'Can you bake the best cupcake? The winner will get a cupcake-shaped trophy. Money from the cupcake sale will help the school.'" She clapped her hands. "I love to bake! I bet I can make a great cupcake!"

"The sale is this Thursday," Mrs. Dawson said. "I'll help you."

Isabel shook her head. "No, Mom. Thanks, but I have to do it myself."

She ran up to her room. Inside her castle, she grabbed a pad of paper and some crayons. She was ready to design the perfect cupcake.

Isabel glanced up at her bookshelf. She imagined a trophy that looked like a shiny cupcake sitting there. She smiled and picked up a bright purple crayon.

"It's time to start my quest!"

Chapter Four

Megan the Bragger

Sunday night, Isabel's dad knocked on her door.

"Come in," Isabel called.

Her dad held a white shoebox in his hands. "I heard about your quest," he said. "Maybe these will help you."

Isabel opened the box. A pair of purple running shoes was tucked inside!

"They were the only purple pair in the store," Mr. Dawson told her. "I hope you like them."

Isabel gave her dad a big hug. "Dad, they're great! I know they'll help me win a prize at Field Day." "Try them on," her dad urged.

Isabel sat in a chair. She put the shoes on her feet, pulled the laces tight, and stood up.

The pretty purple shoes felt loose! But Isabel didn't say that. They were the only pair in the store, and she didn't want to give them back.

"They're perfect," she lied.

Mr. Dawson smiled. "Great, Isabel! I hope they help you win the race."

After her dad left, Isabel started to feel bad about lying. She looked at her feet. Her parents always said she was growing fast.

"Field Day is three weeks away," she said aloud. "Maybe my feet will grow by then."

The next day, Isabel wore her regular white sneakers to school, along with a jean skirt and a purple T-shirt with a star on it. When she got to school, the kids in her class were waiting in line outside.

Her best friends, Mandy and Sandi, waved at her.

"Hi Isabel!" they said at the same time.

Mandy and Sandi were twins. They looked exactly alike. They both had red hair and freckles. They always dressed the same. They even talked at the same time! Isabel had been friends with them since they were all babies, so she could tell them apart. Mandy's eyes were a little bit smaller than Sandi's. And Sandi had more freckles.

"Hi," Isabel said, walking up to the twins. "Guess what? I'm going to enter the Cupcake Contest on Thursday."

Isabel pulled a piece of paper out of her pocket. She showed her friends the cupcake design she had made. The cupcake had purple icing on it. Purple jelly beans decorated the top.

"That's cool, Isabel," Mandy said.

"Super-cool," agreed Sandi.

Then Mandy frowned. "Our mom won't let us enter the contest. She doesn't like it when we eat sugar."

"She says she doesn't want to pay double dentist bills," Sandi added, sighing.

Isabel used to wonder why Mandy always talked first. But the twins said it was because Mandy was born three minutes before Sandy. That made sense to Isabel.

Just then, a girl with blonde hair poked her head between Mandy and Sandi.

"What is that?" asked Megan Carson. She pointed to Isabel's drawing. "It looks like an elephant."

Isabel quickly folded up the piece of paper. "It's a design for my cupcake. I'm going to enter the Cupcake Contest and win the prize."

Megan laughed. "You can't win the prize, because *I* am going to win the prize. I'm making the best cupcake ever. And it does not look like an elephant."

"My cupcake doesn't look like an elephant," Isabel said firmly.

"It does not," Mandy agreed.

"No way!" echoed Sandi.

Then the bell rang, and the kids started to go inside. Megan walked away.

Isabel frowned. Megan could be pretty

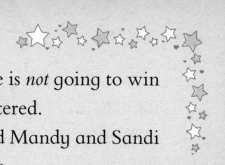

mean sometimes. "She is *not* going to win that contest," she muttered.

"No, she's not," said Mandy and Sandi at the exact same time.

In class, they said the Pledge of Allegiance. Their teacher, Mrs. Lewis, usually started Monday morning with spelling words. But today was different.

"Today we will be doing some creative writing," she said. "That means each of you will write a story."

Some of the kids groaned. They had read lots of stories in class, but they had never made up stories before. Isabel started to feel a little nervous. Would it be hard?

Mrs. Lewis smiled at them. "Don't worry," she said. "We'll start slowly. The first thing you need to do is to come up with an idea."

She showed the class different ways to come up with an idea. That part wasn't

so hard for Isabel. She knew right away that she wanted to write a story about a princess. But what kind of story?

She tapped her pencil on the paper. She wrote down some princess words.

> Princess
>
> Purple
>
> Crown
>
> Prince
>
> Castle

Isabel thought about her own castle. She frowned when she remembered Alex, and how he had stormed her castle.

Then Isabel stopped tapping her pencil. She had an idea!

> The Purple Princess lives in a castle. She has two meen brothers. Her brothers want the castle. The Purple Princess fites to keep her castle safe.

Isabel knew that all the words were not spelled right. But Mrs. Lewis had said that

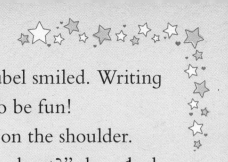

was okay for now. Isabel smiled. Writing this story was going to be fun!

Megan tapped her on the shoulder.

"What's your story about?" she asked. "Is it about a cupcake that looks like an elephant? My story is going to be great."

Isabel didn't answer. Megan thought she was the best at everything! She loved to brag.

But now Isabel knew what she had to do — she had to make the best cupcake ever!

Chapter Five

A Cupcake Disaster

Isabel made her cupcakes on Wednesday night, after dinner. Her mom set all the ingredients out on the table.

First, Isabel made the cupcake batter. Her mom showed her how to use the measuring cups and spoons, but Isabel did everything else herself. She added the flour and sugar and cracked the eggs into the bowl. Then she mixed the batter together. It was a creamy golden color.

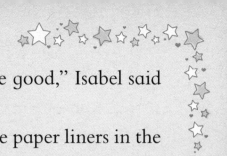

"This is going to be good," Isabel said confidently.

Next, she put purple paper liners in the cupcake pan. Then she poured the batter into the cups.

It was a messy job. Some of the batter spilled onto the pan.

"That's okay," her mom told her. "That always happens." She wiped off the extra batter.

Isabel's mom put the cupcakes into the hot oven. Then she put a chair in front of the oven. She watched the cupcakes bake through the window in the oven door.

"Isabel, you don't have to watch them every second," Mrs. Dawson said.

"Yes, I do," Isabel said firmly. "These cupcakes have to win a prize. I don't want anything bad to happen to them!"

When the timer rang, Mrs. Dawson

took the cupcakes out of the oven and put them on a rack to cool.

Alex ran into the room. "Cupcakes!" he cried. He started to grab one. Isabel jumped in front of him.

"These are *not* for you," she said. "These are for the Cupcake Contest."

"Mooooom!" Alex wailed.

"Isabel is right," Mrs. Dawson said. "Sorry, Alex. We can make cupcakes for us to eat this weekend."

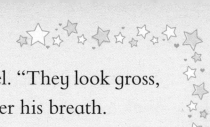

Alex glared at Isabel. "They look gross, anyway," he said under his breath.

"Now it's time to make the icing," their mom said quickly. "You can ice the cupcakes when they cool off, Isabel."

Alex walked away, and Isabel went to the kitchen table. Her mom had bought a tub of plain white icing and some food coloring.

"Did you get purple?" Isabel asked.

Mrs. Dawson shook her head. "They didn't have purple. But you can mix blue and red together to make purple, just like with paint."

Isabel frowned. That sounded kind of hard.

She spooned the white icing into a bowl. Then she put some drops of red food coloring in. Next, she added blue. She stirred them together.

The color didn't look quite like purple.

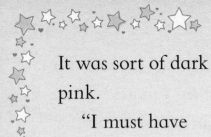

It was sort of dark pink.

"I must have put in too much red," Isabel said. She added more blue. Then she stirred again.

Now the icing looked really blue! Isabel sighed.

"More red," she said. She squeezed the little food coloring bottle.

Splash! A whole bunch of red squirted out.

Isabel stirred and stirred. Now the icing didn't look purple, or pink, or red, or blue. It was a weird shade of brown.

"Mom!" Isabel yelled.

Mrs. Dawson came over to the table and saw the bowl of brownish icing. "Oh," she said.

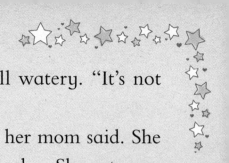

Isabel's eyes got all watery. "It's not purple—it's ugly!"

"It's not that bad," her mom said. She grabbed one of the cupcakes. She put some of the icing on it with a knife. Then she added some purple jelly beans on top. "See? It's pretty," Mrs. Dawson said.

Isabel sniffled. "But it's supposed to be *all* purple. Can we get more icing?"

"Isabel, it's late. It's almost bedtime," Mrs. Dawson said. She unwrapped the frosted cupcake and took a bite. "*Mmm*. It's delicious! That's what's important, isn't it?"

She held it out, and Isabel took a bite, too. It *was* delicious! Maybe Isabel had made the winning cupcakes after all.

"Thanks, Mom," Isabel said.

Isabel and her mom iced and decorated the rest of the cupcakes together. Once they were done, Isabel was feeling pretty good.

Then Marco and Alex ran into the kitchen.

"Yuck! What are those?" Alex asked, pointing.

"They look like mutant cupcakes," Marco said.

"They are not!" Isabel shouted.

"Boys, that's enough," Mrs. Dawson said firmly.

The boys left the kitchen, laughing. Isabel felt like crying all over again.

Her brothers were right. Her cupcakes were a complete disaster!

Chapter Six

And the Trophy Goes To . . .

The next morning after breakfast, Isabel sat on her bed and stared at her bare feet.

"I think they look a *little* bigger," she said to herself.

She put on some purple polka-dotted socks and pulled the purple running shoes out of her closet. She had a feeling they would bring her luck in the Cupcake Contest.

Isabel stepped into the shoes, and her feet slipped around inside. They still didn't fit!

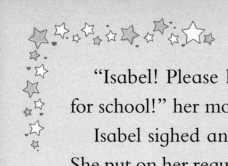

"Isabel! Please hurry—you'll be late for school!" her mom called.

Isabel sighed and pulled off the shoes. She put on her regular white sneakers and ran downstairs.

Mrs. Dawson handed her the box of cupcakes.

"Good luck today, Isabel," she said. "And don't worry if you don't win a prize. You win a prize in my book for working so hard on these cupcakes."

Her mom was being nice, but Isabel knew the truth. Her cupcakes were not going to win. They looked too weird!

"Thanks, Mom," Isabel said sadly.

When Isabel got to school, Mandy and Sandi ran up to her. They both wore big smiles.

"Mom gave us each fifty cents!" Mandy said.

"She said we can each get a cupcake!" Sandi added.

"That's great," Isabel said. But her voice didn't sound happy.

Mandy and Sandi stopped smiling.

"What's the matter?" Mandy asked.

Sandi looked closely at Isabel. "Are you okay?"

Isabel liked having Mandy and Sandi for best friends. They always knew when she was feeling bad. She opened the lid of her cupcake box.

"Look what happened to my cupcakes!"

Mandy and Sandi seemed confused.

"They look like cupcakes," Mandy said, shrugging.

"What's wrong with them?" Sandi asked.

"They're supposed to be purple," Isabel said. "There's nothing special about them. They'll never win a prize!"

Suddenly, the kids around them got very loud. Isabel spun around to see what was going on. She spotted Megan, holding a white box in her hands. A bunch of kids were gathered around her.

"Those are beautiful!" someone said.

"Megan, you'll win the trophy for sure!" said another kid.

Isabel moved closer, until she could see inside the box. Megan had made perfect white cupcakes that looked like fluffy

clouds. Each cupcake was sprinkled with silvery snowflakes and glitter. Isabel hated to admit it, but they *did* look beautiful.

"The snowflakes are made from sugar," Megan said proudly. "I made them all by myself."

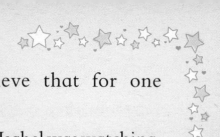

Isabel didn't believe that for one minute.

Megan noticed that Isabel was watching. "Did you bring your elephant cupcakes, Isabel?" she asked in a sweet voice.

"My cupcakes taste delicious, and that's what matters," Isabel said, thinking about what her mom had said.

The bell rang just in time. The kids who had made cupcakes brought them to the assembly room, where parents were setting up the cupcake sale. Then they went to class.

Isabel thought it would be hard to wait until lunch for the Cupcake Contest. Luckily, Mrs. Lewis let them work on their creative writing. Isabel added more to her princess story. She made up an evil fairy named Morgan who turned everything into ice and snow.

Finally, it was time for the contest. All

the kids headed to the assembly room to buy cupcakes.

Isabel had never seen so many cupcakes in her life! Some had flowers on them. Some had silly faces made of candy. Isabel was looking at all the pretty cupcakes when Mandy and Sandi ran up.

Each of the twins had one of Isabel's cupcakes!

"Isabel, this is really good," Mandy said.

"It's delicious," Sandi added.

"Thanks," Isabel said. "But it's not good enough to win."

"Why do you want to win so much?" Mandy asked.

"Yeah, why?" asked Sandi.

"Because of Alex and Marco," Isabel said. "They have lots of trophies, but I don't have any. I'm on a quest to win a prize!"

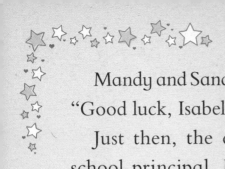

Mandy and Sandi nodded very seriously. "Good luck, Isabel," they said together.

Just then, the crowd got quiet. The school principal, Mrs. Castillo, walked up to the microphone at the front of the room. Isabel noticed that she held the silver cupcake-shaped trophy. It looked amazing!

"Good afternoon, students," the principal said. "Thank you all for making such great cupcakes. It was hard to pick one winner, but the teachers and I have decided."

Isabel held her breath. Her cupcakes *were* delicious. Maybe there was a chance she could win after all!

"The winner is . . . Megan Carson for her snowflake sparkle cupcakes!" Mrs. Castillo announced.

Kids clapped loudly, and Megan squealed with happiness. She ran up to the

microphone. Mrs. Castillo handed her the
trophy.

Isabel felt awful.

"It's okay," Mandy and Sandi said
together.

But it wasn't okay. It wasn't okay at all!

Chapter Seven

A Princess Never Gives Up

Isabel was in a bad mood for the rest of the day. Megan kept the trophy on her desk all afternoon.

When Isabel got home from school, her mom greeted her. "How did it go today?"

"I didn't win," Isabel said sadly. "Megan did."

Mrs. Dawson hugged her. "It's not important who won. What's important is that you tried."

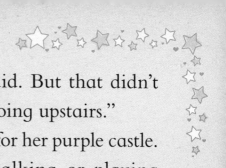

"I guess," Isabel said. But that didn't feel important. "I'm going upstairs."

Isabel headed right for her purple castle. She didn't feel like talking or playing outside. All she wanted to do was forget about the Cupcake Contest!

Isabel snuggled into the pillows and turned on the lamp. She picked up *The Magic Jewel* and began to read.

The story was getting good. Princess Crystal had left her castle and started her quest. Then she came to a high mountain. It was so high she couldn't climb it. Princess Crystal almost gave up.

"I am a princess, and a princess never gives up," Crystal said.

Then she went to a cave and made friends with a giant bird there. The bird agreed to fly her up the mountain.

Isabel stared at the picture in the book for a while. Princess Crystal sat on the

back of the beautiful golden bird. Crystal's long hair flowed behind her. She looked really happy.

A princess never gives up.

"Princess Crystal almost gave up," Isabel said out loud. "But she didn't."

She closed the book with a thud. "I won't give up, either! I will finish my quest."

She came out of the castle and changed into her purple shoes. Then she ran downstairs.

"Where are you going?" her mom asked.

"To practice for Field Day," Isabel shouted behind her.

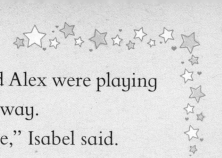

Outside, Marco and Alex were playing basketball in the driveway.

"Hey, Alex, race me," Isabel said.

"What for?" Alex asked.

"I need to practice," Isabel said. "Are you afraid I'll beat you?"

Alex tossed the basketball aside. "Okay. To the end of the driveway and back. Ready?" He and Isabel lined up on a crack in the pavement.

"Ready?" Marco asked. "One, two, three—go!"

Isabel and Alex charged down the driveway. The purple shoes still felt loose on Isabel's feet, but she ran fast anyway. She reached the end of the driveway first and turned around.

But on the way back to the starting line, Alex sped up. He beat her by just a few feet!

"I won!" Alex cheered.

"But not by much," Marco pointed out.

Alex frowned. "So what?"

Mrs. Dawson came out of the house. "Isabel, what are you wearing on your feet?" she asked.

Isabel looked down at her purple sneakers. "Dad gave them to me."

Her mom walked up and examined them. She shook her head. "Isabel, those are

too big. Go put on your white sneakers."

Isabel raced upstairs. She threw the purple shoes in her closet, put on her white sneakers, and dashed back to the front yard.

"Alex, race me again," she said.

"Sure," Alex said with a smirk. "You must like losing."

They lined up again.

"One, two, three—go!" Marco cried.

Isabel didn't have to worry about her feet sliding around this time. She ran faster than before. She reached the end of the driveway first again. But this time, Alex didn't catch up.

"Isabel wins!" Marco announced. He sounded a little surprised.

Alex scowled. "So what? I beat her before."

"That's because I was wearing the wrong sneakers," Isabel said. "Now you'll

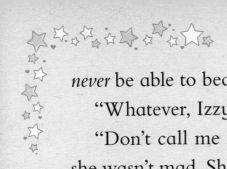

never be able to beat me!"

"Whatever, Izzy," Alex mumbled.

"Don't call me Izzy!" Isabel said. But she wasn't mad. She felt great! Alex was a good runner, and he was two years older than her. If she could beat Alex, she could beat the other girls in second grade.

For the first time, Isabel felt absolutely sure of it: She was going to win a prize!

Chapter Eight

The Lost Sneakers

The next week, Isabel finished writing her story and handed it in to Mrs. Lewis. In the story, the Purple Princess defeated the bad snow fairy. She fought her brothers. She kept her kingdom safe. And of course, she lived happily ever after.

At home, Isabel practiced running every day. Alex wouldn't race her anymore. He was still mad about losing. But Marco raced her sometimes. Even though she couldn't beat him, it was good practice.

Other days, her dad timed her with a stopwatch.

Then it was finally Field Day! The morning was bright and sunny. Isabel jumped out of bed and put on a pair of purple shorts and a purple T-shirt. Then she ran downstairs to eat breakfast.

Mrs. Dawson put a bowl of cereal in front of her. "It's got whole grains in it. It will give you energy for your race."

Alex walked into the kitchen. He looked grumpy. "What's the big deal about Isabel's race?"

"It's a big deal because I'm going to win," Isabel said.

Alex sat down. He ate his cereal fast.

"You're hungry this morning!" Mrs. Dawson said, raising her eyebrows.

"Maybe I'm getting ready for a race too," Alex grumbled. He stood up, put his bowl in the sink, and headed back to his room.

Isabel finished her cereal. She brushed her teeth and then went upstairs to get her white sneakers. But when she looked in her closet, they weren't there.

"Mom!" Isabel yelled. "I can't find my sneakers!"

Isabel's mom helped her take all of the shoes out of her closet. They looked in the downstairs coat closet. They looked in the garage. But they couldn't find the sneakers anywhere.

"Oh Isabel, I'm afraid you're going to have to wear those purple sneakers or 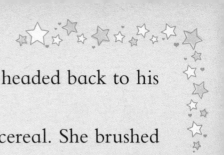 you'll be late to school," Mrs. Dawson said. "Tie the laces tightly. If I find your white sneakers, I'll bring them to Field Day. Okay?"

Isabel nodded. She put on her purple sneakers. They still felt loose, but Isabel wasn't too worried.

At least they're purple! she thought. *Maybe they'll bring me luck.*

At school, all of the kids were excited about Field Day. Outside, each class sat together on the bleachers.

Mrs. Lewis told Isabel's class about the plan for the day. "You can each participate in one event," she said. "You will be competing against other girls and boys in second grade."

The kids lined up in front of Mrs. Lewis to sign up for events. Mandy and Sandi decided to do the three-legged race. When it was Isabel's turn to sign up, she asked a question.

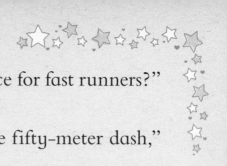

"What's a good race for fast runners?" she asked.

"You should try the fifty-meter dash," Mrs. Lewis said.

Isabel nodded. Mrs. Lewis wrote her name on the chart.

Finally, it was time for Field Day to start! Isabel sat with Mandy and Sandi and watched the first graders' events.

"I'm so nervous," Isabel said.

"Don't be," Mandy told her.

"You're fast, Isabel," Sandi added.

Megan leaned forward from her spot on the bleachers. "Oh, are you entering the fifty-meter dash, Isabel?" she asked.

"Yes, I am," Isabel answered. "I've been practicing."

"Me too," Megan said. "I hope I win. The Field Day trophy will look nice next to my cupcake trophy."

With a big smile, Megan turned to talk to one of her friends.

Isabel frowned. "She always brags so much!" she said. "I hope I beat her."

"Me, too!" said Mandy and Sandi.

Then a loud whistle cut through the air.

"Okay second grade, you're up!" Mrs. Lewis called out.

The three-legged race was first, so Mandy and Sandi headed to the field. The racers worked in pairs. Mrs. Lewis tied Mandy's right leg to Sandi's left leg. They practiced walking.

"This is easy," the twins said.

When the race began, Isabel cheered them on. Some of the other kids had trouble walking together, but Mandy and Sandi were fast. They were the first to cross the finish line.

"Yay! Go, Mandy and Sandi!" Isabel cheered.

Mr. G., the gym teacher, gave Mandy and Sandi each a tiny trophy. Mrs. Lewis untied their legs, and they ran up to Isabel, smiling.

"That was fun!" Mandy said.

"I wish we could do it again," Sandi added.

But then Isabel heard Mrs. Lewis make a very important announcement. "It's time for the girls' fifty-meter dash!"

Isabel walked up to the starting line. Megan was there, along with Sophia and Lily from the other second grade class.

Isabel tried not to be nervous. She looked around, hoping to spot her mom with her white sneakers, but she was nowhere to be seen. So Isabel stretched out her legs, like her dad had taught her. She checked her shoelaces to make sure they were nice and tight.

"Everybody ready?" Mr. G. asked.

"Ready!" the four girls called out.

"On your mark, get set, go!"

Isabel took off. She looked straight ahead at the finish line. She ran as fast as she could. Her sneakers still felt loose, but she tried to ignore them.

Isabel heard lots of yelling and cheering around her. Then, out of the corner of her eye, she saw that Megan was catching up to her.

The finish line was not far away. Isabel pushed herself faster. She was determined to win!

Suddenly, her right sneaker flew off! Isabel almost tripped, but she steadied herself and kept running.

She couldn't run fast enough in just one sneaker, though. Megan passed her—and crossed the finish line first!

"Megan wins!" somebody shouted.

Isabel came in second place. She stopped, trying to catch her breath. Then

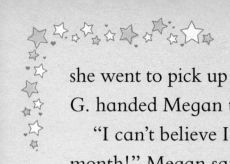

she went to pick up her sneaker while Mr. G. handed Megan the trophy.

"I can't believe I won two trophies this month!" Megan said loudly.

Isabel tried not to cry. But it was so hard. She walked back to the bleachers and covered her face with her hands, hoping no one would see.

Mandy and Sandi sat down on either side of her.

"Isabel, that was so unfair," Mandy said.

Sandi nodded. "You should have won."

Isabel wiped the tears from her face. "It doesn't matter," she said, sniffling. "I don't care about winning a trophy anymore. My quest is over!"

Chapter Nine

Into the Dark Forest

Isabel did not have much fun for the rest of Field Day. Not even when the teachers had a water balloon fight. Not even when everyone got ice pops. Not even a *purple* ice pop could make Isabel happy.

When Isabel and her brothers got home from school, Mrs. Dawson looked unhappy, too. She was standing on the front steps, holding Isabel's white sneakers.

"Where did you find them?" Isabel asked.

"I think we need to ask Alex that question," Mrs. Dawson said.

Alex looked down at the ground.

"Alex, did you take Isabel's sneakers?" she asked.

"Yes," he mumbled.

Isabel gasped. "Alex, that is the meanest thing you have ever done!" she said.

"We all need to talk about this," Mrs. Dawson said, looking from Isabel to Alex.

"I DON'T FEEL LIKE TALKING!" Isabel shouted. She ran inside and went right up to her castle. Isabel threw herself on her purple pillows and cried.

Alex was so mean! It was all his fault

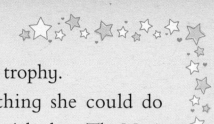

that she didn't have a trophy.

But there was nothing she could do about that now. Isabel picked up *The Magic Jewel* and started to read.

Princess Crystal said good-bye to the golden bird. She climbed down the mountain and entered a dark, dark, forest. She got very lost there.

"I know that princesses never give up," Princess Crystal said. *"But I feel like giving up now."*

"I know how you feel," Isabel said.

Isabel kept on reading. Princess Crystal kept going.

"My quest is not over," Crystal said.

Soon she saw a light glowing in the darkness. She got close to it. The light was coming from a beautiful jewel!

"I have found it!" said Princess Crystal. *"I have found the magic jewel!"*

Isabel heard a knock on her door. When she pulled back her purple curtain, she saw her mom come into the room. Alex and Marco were behind her. Alex had his hands behind his back.

"Alex has something to say to you," Mrs. Dawson told Isabel.

"Isabel, I'm sorry," Alex said. "I was mad that you beat me. Everyone made a big deal about your race. I was jealous."

"I was jealous of you, too," Isabel said. "You and Marco have all those trophies.

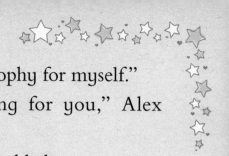

All I wanted was a trophy for myself."

"I made something for you," Alex said.

"I helped," Marco added.

Alex held out his hands. He was holding a trophy! It looked like it had been made from a cereal box.

Isabel came out of her castle. She looked at the trophy. There was writing on it.

Isabel Dawson: World's Greatest Sister.

Isabel couldn't help smiling. The trophy wasn't a magic jewel . . . but it was even better!

Chapter Ten

The Prize Surprise

Isabel put the trophy on her bookshelf. It looked awesome.

The next day, Isabel didn't feel so sad. Not even when Megan started bragging about Field Day.

"Hi, Isabel. Sorry you lost the race yesterday," Megan said, walking up to Isabel in the hallway.

Mandy and Sandi put their hands on their hips.

"It's only because her sneaker fell off," Mandy said.

Sandi nodded. "Yeah. She was winning!"

"That's okay," Isabel said. "There will be another Field Day next year. And next time, my sneakers will fit."

Isabel walked right past Megan into the classroom.

Once everyone had settled down, Mrs. Lewis stood in front of the class. She had a huge grin on her face.

"I have a big surprise for someone in our class today," she announced. "I liked the stories you wrote so much, I entered them in a contest. And one of the stories won a prize!"

Everyone got excited. They started to chatter. Megan leaned over to her friend Kayla.

"I'll bet it's me," Megan said in a loud whisper.

Isabel tried not to pay attention, but Megan was probably right. She always won everything.

Mrs. Lewis picked up something from her desk. It looked like a picture frame.

"I am happy to say that the winner is . . . Isabel Dawson," the teacher said.

Isabel was shocked! Everyone clapped.

"Come up here, Isabel," Mrs. Lewis told her.

Isabel slowly walked up to the front of the room. She felt like she was in a dream. Mrs. Lewis gave her the picture frame.

Inside was a fancy certificate. Isabel read the words on it.

State Library Writing Contest
Winner, Fiction, Age 7
Isabel Dawson, for
"The Purple Princess"

"You won, Isabel," Mrs. Lewis said. "Your story was the best of all the seven-year-olds who entered the contest."

"I really won?" Isabel asked. She still couldn't believe it.

Mrs. Lewis nodded. "You sure did."

"Yay, Isabel!" Mandy and Sandi cheered.

Everyone clapped again—even Megan. "I guess I can't win *all* the trophies," she muttered.

Isabel stared at the certificate all day. It was just a piece of paper with writing on it. But to Isabel, it was better than a shiny trophy or even a glowing jewel.

When she got home, she showed the certificate to her mom. Alex and Marco were there too.

"Isabel, I'm so proud of you!" Mrs. Dawson said. "Dad is going to love this."

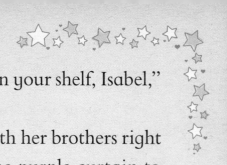

"You should put it on your shelf, Isabel," Alex said.

She ran upstairs, with her brothers right behind. She opened the purple curtain to her castle.

"You may come in," she told Alex and Marco, in her best princess voice.

Isabel looked for a place on her

State Library Writing Contest

★ *Winner, Fiction, Age 7* ★
Isabel Dawson
for
The Purple Princess

shelf to put the certificate. The trophy Alex had made took up a lot of room. And her princess figures were already squished together.

"I think you need another shelf," Alex suggested.

Isabel smiled. "You're right!" she said. "I need to make room for all of the other prizes I'm going to win!"

Make It Yourself!
Sparkly Crown Bookmark

Isabel loves to read books. Now you can make a princess bookmark to keep your place when *you're* reading! You need:

- ruler
- 1 piece of purple card stock
- 1 piece of gold card stock
- stick-on gems
- scissors
- glue stick
- pencil

1. Use the ruler to make a rectangle on the purple card stock. It should be 6 inches long and 1-½ inches wide. Cut it out.

2. On the gold card stock, draw a crown that is 2-½ inches wide, with three points on top. Cut it out.

3. Trace the crown on the leftover gold card stock. Now cut out this new crown, so you have two crowns that are exactly alike.

4. Glue the first crown to the purple strip, about ½ inch from the top. Flip it over, and glue the other crown to the other side of the bookmark so that it lines up with the first crown.

5. Decorate one side of the crown with stick-on gems to make a tiara fit for a princess. Time to read!

Don't miss another royal
adventure—look for

Green
Princess
Saves the
Day

Turn the page for
a special sneak peek!

"Do we have to go already?" Holly Greenwood asked her sister.

Jessica rolled her eyes. "I don't know why you think this park is so great."

"It's the best park in the world!" Holly said, stretching her arms out to the sides.

Jessica took Holly's hand and headed down the path. Holly smiled as an orange butterfly flew past them.

When they got to the end of the path, Holly stopped. A big sign was sticking out of the grass. It said, FOR SALE.

Jessica walked up to the sign. "Wow," she said. "It looks like the park is for sale."

Holly wasn't sure she heard right. "The whole park?"

Jessica nodded. "The town is trying to sell it and turn it into a shopping center."

"They can't!" Holly cried. She couldn't believe it.

Who would want to get rid of the most beautiful park in the world?